MYTHS UNTOLD

Stories From The Golden Past, Retold In The Present

Anannya Dwivedi

Wordly Wise Publishers

Published by
Wordly Wise Publishers & Distributors
3rd Floor, 44, Regal Building,
Hanuman Road Area, Connaught Place,
New Delhi 110001
+91-9836325999

Email – hello@wordlywise.co.in

The illustrations are prompt generated.

ISBN : 978-93-94075-60-3
First impression (2024)

MYTHS UNTOLD

Stories From The Golden Past, Retold In The Present

Wordly Wise Publishers

Contents

Acknowledgements

Thank You

To my Grandpa, my first teacher.

To my Grandma, whose childhood stories sparked my imagination.

To my Dad, a constant voice of encouragement to read and imagine.

To my Mom, my biggest supporter, full of unconditional love.

To Meeta Aunty, the artist who brought my characters to life with her beautiful illustrations

To Chandni Aunty and team Wordly Wise Publishers, the team that helped me get this book to you.

To my school and teachers, who gave me the right exposure and encouragement.

To my dear friends, my constant supporters.

And to the Almighty, whose blessings have made this journey possible.

Prologue

Let me begin by answering a question that many of you may have: Why did I name my stories this way, and what is their context?

Growing up, I was always curious to know the reason behind everything. Living with my grandparents, interacting with my extended family, and having access to books, I was told many stories that somehow had a pattern. The donkey was dumb, the fox was clever, and the crow was thirsty. The stepmother was evil & the Brahmin was always poor. Mumma told me that these were biases conveyed through stories over the years. I told her I didn't understand why it should be this way.

There were many beliefs that I came across in stories and also in everyday life that heightened my curiosity- If someone asked where the other person was going, why was it considered bad? Why was it considered wrong if someone sneezed before starting any work? Why was a cat crossing someone's path considered unlucky while someone having itchy palms was considered lucky? Mumma told me these beliefs were called superstitions, as they have been told through stories and shared experiences over generations.

I often wondered – what if those stories and experiences were positive? Maybe people wouldn't mind if a cat crossed their path if I changed their beliefs.

So, at the age of nine, I decided to write new stories that could convey the same old stories in a positive way, without biases and superstitions. That's how Myths Untold was born! I hope you enjoy reading this book and have new stories to tell everyone from here on.

Happy Reading!!
Anannya

The Clever
Donkey

Once upon a time, there lived a lonely washerman. His only companion was his beloved donkey. They were very good friends. One day, the washerman had to go to the city. So, he packed his belongings and set out.

On his way, the washerman had to cross a Forest. He was walking leisurely when he suddenly fell into a patch of quicksand.

“Help! Help!”, he shouted.
His donkey got worried and thought of a plan to rescue his master. He then saw an old log of wood. Gathering all of his strength, he started pulling the log towards the ditch and threw it towards his master. The washerman climbed onto the log and pulled himself out.

He then said to the donkey, “I have heard all my life that donkeys are dumb, but you have taught me that donkeys are Smart. Not only that; they have a great heart too. From now onwards, you are my son, because the way you rescued me is how a son would save his father. God bless you.” Since then, they both developed a beautiful relationship of a father and son.

The Good Stepmother

Once upon a time in the palace of Kamalapur, there lived a princess called Bhavini. She was six years old and was very beautiful, kind, and loving. One day, the Queen of Kamalapur fell very ill. Many doctors were called in to check on her but no one could find a cure. The illness eventually got to her and she passed away. The kingdom was in complete dismay.

Soon, the king decided to marry another woman. The new Queen was very sweet and pretty and loved Bhavini like her own daughter. Bhavini missed her mother but loved her new stepmother too.

One Day Bhavini got really sick. The Queen showered her with a lot of care and love. Together, they battled the illness, and their bond grew stronger than ever.

Bhavini & her stepmother built a deep relationship of love and care. The whole Kingdom talked about it fondly. It showed everyone that step-mothers need not necessarily be bad as we have heard in other stories.

The Lucky
Walk Of
The Cat

Once upon a time, there was a man called Venkat who lived in a village in Kerala. He had a coconut business and refused to let any cat enter his farm of coconuts because he believed that cats were unlucky and would cause him misfortune.

One day, his neighbour Surjeeth saw him working. He had always been very jealous of Venkat so he let a black cat into his farm on his way home. When Venkat saw the cat roaming on his farm, he was angered and went home in disappointment. His wife, Bhagya, asked him what had happened, and he told her the whole story. Just then, Venkat's phone rang - it was his mother who lived in Munnar. "How are you, amma?"" he said.

"Venkat!" she exclaimed excitedly, "The disease I was suffering from has been cured by eating food cooked in the oil made from the coconuts from your farm. The doctor said that the oil I was having earlier was unhealthy and was being cooked wrongly."

Venkat was very happy to see that his mother was fine now. It was then that he realised the potential the coconut oil had and he immediately called some of his business partners to discuss launching oil as a product for cooking. They all began working on mass-producing the oil for consumption.

The next day onwards, orders started to pour in. His coconut oil business got some big clients and started doing very well. Everything was going great for Venkat, but he couldn't stop thinking about that black cat and wondered if it really meant bad luck. He then eventually realised that so much good had happened to him despite the black cat crossing his way. He began rethinking his older beliefs.

He discussed his thoughts with his wife who gently smiled and agreed, "You are absolutely right"she said, nodding her head., "The belief was wrong, and if anything, the cat's walk only turned out to be auspicious for us. Fortune favours the brave, I guess!"

Venkat acknowledged it with a smile and started planning for his next project. Since then, his coconut farm has always welcomed cats from all over the village!

The Satisfied Crow

Once upon a time, there lived a kind girl named Kaveri who loved birds. One day, a crow came and sat on her window sill. Kaveri thought he was thirsty and gave him a bowl of fresh water. Since then, the crow would come daily and have water from the bowl she kept for him.

One day, Kaveri asked him, "How come you are always thirsty?" To her surprise, the crow replied, "It's not water that I am thirsty for," and flew away.

The next day, when Kaveri kept the water in the bowl, the crow didn't show up. A few days passed but Kaveri's bowl of water was left untouched. She got sad and checked with her mother, "Maa, why has the crow stopped coming to me?"

Her mom replied, "Kaveri, what the crow was trying to tell you was that he wasn't there for water; he was there for you and your care.

When you asked him that question, he probably got hurt. As far as water is concerned, the crow was satisfied".

That day onwards, Kaveri started to keep the water bowl along with a sorry note for the crow. And then finally, one fine morning, the crow showed up, overlooked the bowl of water, picked the note in his beak and flew away. The crow returned the next day and spoke to Kaveri, and a new friendship blossomed.

A
Valuable Piece
of Trash

Once upon a time, in a small village, there lived a poor orphaned man called Kaushik. He used to clean garbage at the train station to make a living.

Kaushik loved to solve mysteries and wanted to be a detective some day. One day, he was cleaning the platform when he saw a piece of paper lying there as trash. He picked it up, and found a train ticket for somebody named Ranu Singh. It had a strange impression of a coin on it which made Kaushik very suspicious.

He had heard that a lot of gold was stolen from the king's treasury and the king had declared to give 1 lakh gold coins to the person who caught the thief. Kaushik ran to the king's court and showed the strange paper to the king. The king said, "Oh my god! This impression belonged to the most special coin that I had. This was the one coin that no other king had!" Kaushik immediately got to know that Ranu Singh was the thief.

The King sent his soldiers and got Ranu Singh arrested Immediately. Kaushik was rewarded 1 lakh gold coins; with which he opened a school and educated the kids of the village.

Kaushik's School

The
Not-So-Clever
Fox

Once upon a time in a dense jungle located in South America, there lived a fox. She was always extremely proud of how clever she was.

One day, she saw a little rabbit collecting carrots for a feast in his family. She thought of tricking the rabbit and eating him up for dinner. She went to him and said, "I want to have you for dinner. Leave all of this, I will eat you."

The rabbit said, "Okay, but I am just one rabbit. I know a place where there are a lot more rabbits. It is near the lion's den. Please go and hunt them first and then me." The fox agreed and went quickly.

When she reached near the lion's den, she shouted, "I know all of you are hiding here. Now come out and become my feast tonight."

The lion in the den next to her was hungry as he had just gotten up from his sleep. He came out, grabbed the fox, took her to his den, and ate her up.

So, you see, kids, foxes are not always clever. Sometimes, they can be tricked by more clever creatures, like the rabbit in our story.

Spilled Milk That Brought Fortune

Once upon a time, there lived a king named Dharmendra. He had a minister called Sujit. He was evil and wanted to kill the king to take over the throne.

One day, the king ordered the minister to get him some hot milk. The minister thought of poisoning the milk. He bribed the maid for a ransom of 1000 gold coins and asked her to poison it. The maid did as she was told.

When the maid was cooking for the rest of the family, she didn't notice that the milk had boiled over so much that it started spilling all over the kitchen counter. Before she could notice, the queen came and saw this. She was furious and shouted at the maid.

She said, "You fool, don't you know that spilling milk is so inauspicious!". Before the maid could clean up, the queen's pet cat came and started to drink the milk on the counter.

As soon as the cat did that, she immediately died. The king was now aware that the maid had poisoned the milk. When questioned, she revealed that it was done on behalf of the minister. Both of them got jailed.

Later, the queen and king realized that if the milk hadn't spilled and the cat hadn't drunk it, they would never have known the minister's intentions. So, the spilled milk ended up actually being auspicious for the king, the queen, and their family.

The Auspicious Sneeze

Once upon a time, there lived a rude woman called Janaki. She used to always make a fuss about little things. One day, her husband, Prakash, had to go out of town to look for a job. Janaki was very stressed about whether or not he would get the job. So she performed all the rituals she knew of but something happened later, that got her really upset.

Their neighbour had a dog called Kaali who was very fond of Prakash. Janaki, however, was allergic to dogs. When her husband started to leave, the dog came near Janaki. She could not control herself and sneezed due to allergy.

Janaki believed that sneezing, when somebody is stepping out of their house, is a bad omen. However, Prakash was getting late for his train that evening and quickly left. Janaki was worried and shooed away the dog angrily. She kept thinking about the incident. She did not eat or drink anything during the day.

After a few days, her husband returned. Anxiously, she asked him, "Dear, did you get the job?" Her husband smiled and replied, "Of course I did!" Janaki started to cry, "But,

I sneezed right before you left that day!" she replied. "Yes, you did. But so what?" he questioned," I got the job because they found me suitable for the role.

It's a job in a veterinary hospital and the amount of time I spent with our neighbour's dog Kaali helped me answer some very relevant questions on the subject." Janaki realized she was being superstitious and from that day onwards grew very affectionate towards Kaali.

The Rich Brahmin

Once upon a time, there lived a Brahmin who was known in the village for his deep knowledge about rituals. One day, he was called to a house to perform a puja. When he reached there, he saw that the puja was held by a very rich businessman for his daughter's birthday. So, he went and performed the puja. After a while, it was time for the Dakshina. He went to the rich businessman and asked for it. The rich businessman thanked him for his blessings and gave him a lot of money in return. He was overjoyed.

The next month, Brahmin's friend came to visit him. He saw how rich the Brahmin had become and asked him, "From the last time I came to your house, it looks very beautiful. What is the reason?" The Brahmin replied, "I went to a rich businessman's house and performed a puja. In the Dakshina, he gave me a lot of money". The Brahmin's friend got jealous and decided to meet the wealthy businessman. So, he went to his house and asked the businessman about any upcoming pujas, and found out that the businessman was having a puja the month after. He asked the businessman if he could perform the rituals at the ceremony.

The businessman agreed and they made a deal. On the day of the puja, the Brahmin's friend went to the businessman's house and hurriedly did the puja, eagerly waiting for the Dakshina to come.

After the puja, when the time of the Dakshina came, the businessman gave him only a little money. The Brahmin's friend got offended and said, " What are you doing? You gave my friend so much money and you're giving me so little?"

The businessman said, "Sir, your friend had real devotion and performed the most elaborate and detailed puja I had ever seen. He did not care about his Dakshina; he only cared about the puja. That's why I gave him more money. You were in a hurry to finish the puja and therefore, I am giving you the amount that you deserve for the devotion you put into the puja. Your friend is not rich because of the money I gave him – he is rich because he is fully devoted to his work". The Brahmin's friend realized his mistake and stopped being greedy.

The Lucky
Prompt

Once upon a time, there lived a King named Maurya. King Maurya's wife was Queen Mayavati. He also had a minister called Chandra. He envied King Maurya very much and wanted to take over the throne by aligning himself with Maurya's brother.

The king's father had split the kingdom between the king and his brother before he passed away. However, his evil brother had ended up taking more than his share. Maurya went to him many times and tried to claim his share but his brother never agreed to it. This time, Maurya thought he had enough and decided to go for a war against his brother.

Chandra thought of an evil plan to breach King Maurya's confidence by doing something inauspicious for the king since he knew Maurya and Mayavati were very superstitious. So, when Maurya was going out on the day

of the war, Chandra decided to trick the king. Where are you going, sir?" He questioned, innocently. The king was furious at Chandra for he believed it was an ill omen to ask someone about where one was going before leaving the house, but he just rushed out as he was getting late.

Mayavati, who was equally superstitious, was disappointed and angry. After a few days, when the king returned home, he had great news - he had won the war and gotten his share of the kingdom. The queen was both shocked and happy at the same time. The minister was furious that his plan had failed.

Later, the king and queen discussed and understood that the king won the war because he fairly fought for what was rightfully his. So they stopped believing in any superstitions, thereafter. They also understood Chandra's ill intent and sent him into exile. After that Maurya ruled the kingdom peacefully for many years.

The False Caw
Of The Crow

Once upon a time in a village near the city of Pune, there lived a farmer called Siddharth. He was very hardworking and lived a happy life. His wife, Sushma, was a very cheerful and kind lady.

One day, Sidharth was waiting for a businessman who was coming to buy his crops. He was waiting for him at the doorstep. His wife heard the crow cawing and she said "Dear, the crow is cawing, that means the businessman is coming." The farmer was happy, and they waited eagerly for the businessman. They waited till evening but nobody came. Sad and heartbroken, eventually, they went inside.

A few days later there was a knock at the door. Siddharth's wife opened the door and, to everyone's surprise, it was the businessman.

They welcomed him joyfully and he ended up buying a lot of crops from them and gave them a lot of money in return. From that day onwards, Siddharth lived a happy life with Sushma and they looked forward to unexpected guests; whether the crow cawed or not.

No Money
With Itchy
Palms

Once upon a time, there lived a rich miser named Bishwajeet who lived with his wife Shobha and daughter Neha. Bishwajeet was very greedy and superstitious. He used to love it when his palms itched because that meant his business would go well that day and he would earn lot of money.

One day, when his palms itched, he was very happy. He said to his wife, "Shobha, today I am very happy. My palms are itching! I am going to make a lot of money today." Shobha hated this habit of her husband. She stayed quiet and gave him a gentle smile.

When Biswajeet came back home that day, he looked sad. Shobha asked him about what had happened. "Well," he replied, "because my palms were itching today, I was hoping to make a lot of money. In that haste, I did a quick trade with a local merchant without checking his background.

That person was later caught by the police for being involved in wrong practices and I lost all my money". His wife said, "Superstitions don't get you results ;you get results through hard work and intelligence". So, from that day onwards, Bishwajeet started working hard and succeeded in his business. He completely stopped believing in superstitions.

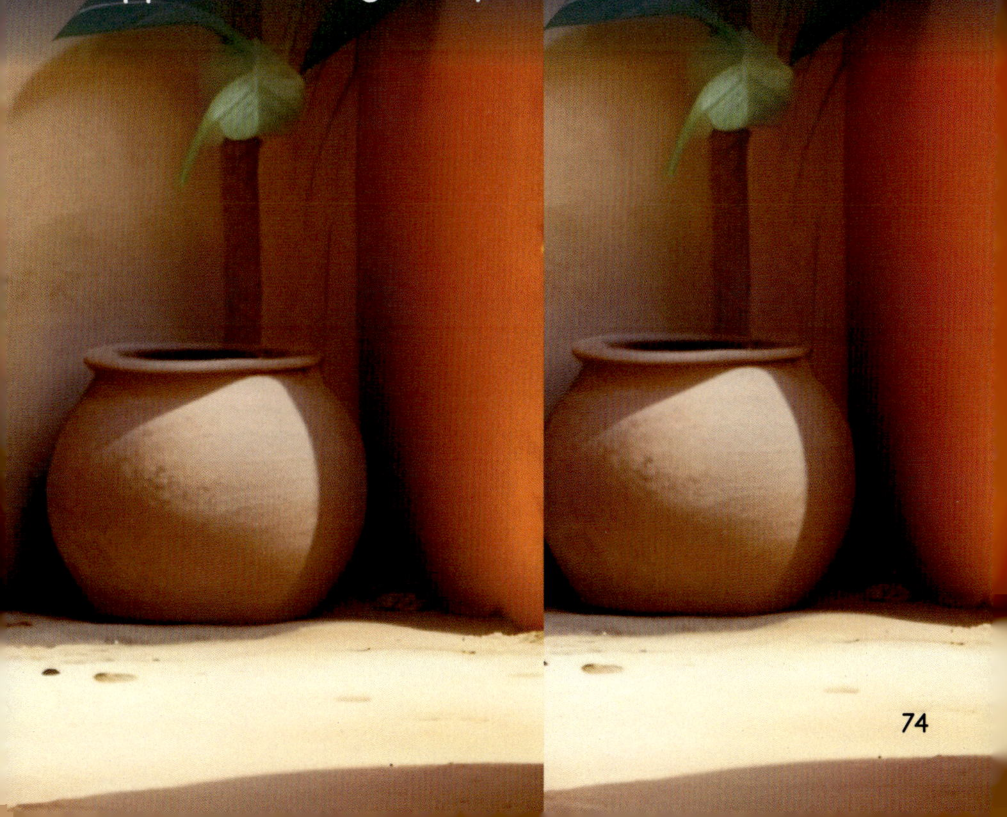

The lucky
Number 13

Once upon a time, there lived a little girl named Avishka. She was 11 years old and used to study in the 6th standard. She used to love collecting stamps.

One day, she thought of putting up a stamp stall in her society. She was working out the cost of each stamp and then asked her mom if one stamp could cost Rs 13. Her mother declined and said, “Avishka, 13 is an unlucky number, so please do not use that number anywhere ever” Avishka agreed, and from that day onwards, she started believing that 13 was an unlucky number.

After a few months, Avishka had her exams coming up, so she started studying really hard. On the day of the exam, she was worried when she saw that her friend Saanvi's roll number was 13. Saanvi had studied very hard this time. Avishka told her that 13 is an unlucky number and that she might get low marks. Saanvi got sad but still gave her best in the exam.

When the results were declared, Saanvi ended up topping the class. She was overjoyed. That was the day Avishka realised that no superstition can decide your result. It's your hard work that decides it instead. From then on, Avishka started to treat 13 as a normal number.